Baby Dragon

Baby Dragon

Amy Ehrlich   *illustrated by* Will Hillenbrand

CANDLEWICK PRESS
CAMBRIDGE, MASSACHUSETTS

One afternoon, Baby Dragon's mother said,
"Grandma is not feeling well. I must go see her."

She warmed Baby Dragon's face and tickled his tail.
They were on the riverbank.

"Wait for me by this red fern," she said. "I'll be back
by morning."

Baby Dragon waited.

He drew a picture in the dirt.

He counted his claws.

He took a nap.

Then Frog hopped by.

"What are you doing?" Frog asked.

"I'm waiting for my mother," said Baby Dragon.

"Don't wait," said Frog. "Come and play."

"No," said Baby Dragon. "If I come with you, my mother won't be able to find me."

"Then good-bye," said Frog. And he hopped away.

Baby Dragon looked all around.
He could not see his mother anywhere.

He nibbled some grass.

He caught a mosquito.

He took a nap.

"What are you doing?" Weasel asked.

"I'm waiting for my mother," said Baby Dragon.

"Don't wait," said Weasel. "I know where we can find ripe bananas to eat. I'll take you there."

"No," said Baby Dragon. "If I come with you, my mother won't be able to find me."

"Then good-bye," said Weasel. And she crept away.

Baby Dragon sang himself a song:

"I want my mother.

I want her now.

I want to warm her face—

and how!"

Baby Dragon looked all around,
but he still could not see his mother.
She said she'd be back by morning.
When would morning come?

As Baby Dragon thought about his mother, he got
sadder and sadder. He was even too sad to take a nap.

Then Crocodile glided by.

"What are you doing?" Crocodile asked.

"I'm waiting for my mother," said Baby Dragon.

"Jump on my back," said Crocodile. "I'll take you to find her."

Baby Dragon looked all around.

The sun was setting. The trees were black against the sky. But he still could not see his mother.

Crocodile was waiting.

Baby Dragon closed his eyes tight and jumped onto Crocodile's back.

Night birds called as they glided up the river.

Crocodile swam for a long time with Baby Dragon
on his back.

Baby Dragon looked at the shore.

He saw rocks and turtles and water buffalo, but
he did not see his mother.

Then the wind came up and sang to Baby Dragon
in his mother's voice:

"Wait here. I'll be back.

I'll be back by morning."

"STOP!" said Baby Dragon to Crocodile. "I want to
go back and wait for my mother."

But Crocodile only laughed.

"Oh, no," he said. "I am taking you to my swamp
up the river. I am going to feed you to my children."

Baby Dragon knew he had to be brave.
He waited until Crocodile swam near
a log. Then he closed his eyes
tight and JUMPED.

The log slipped. Baby Dragon
almost fell into the water.

But he held on tight and paddled the log to shore.
Crocodile kept swimming. He did not know that Baby
Dragon had gone.

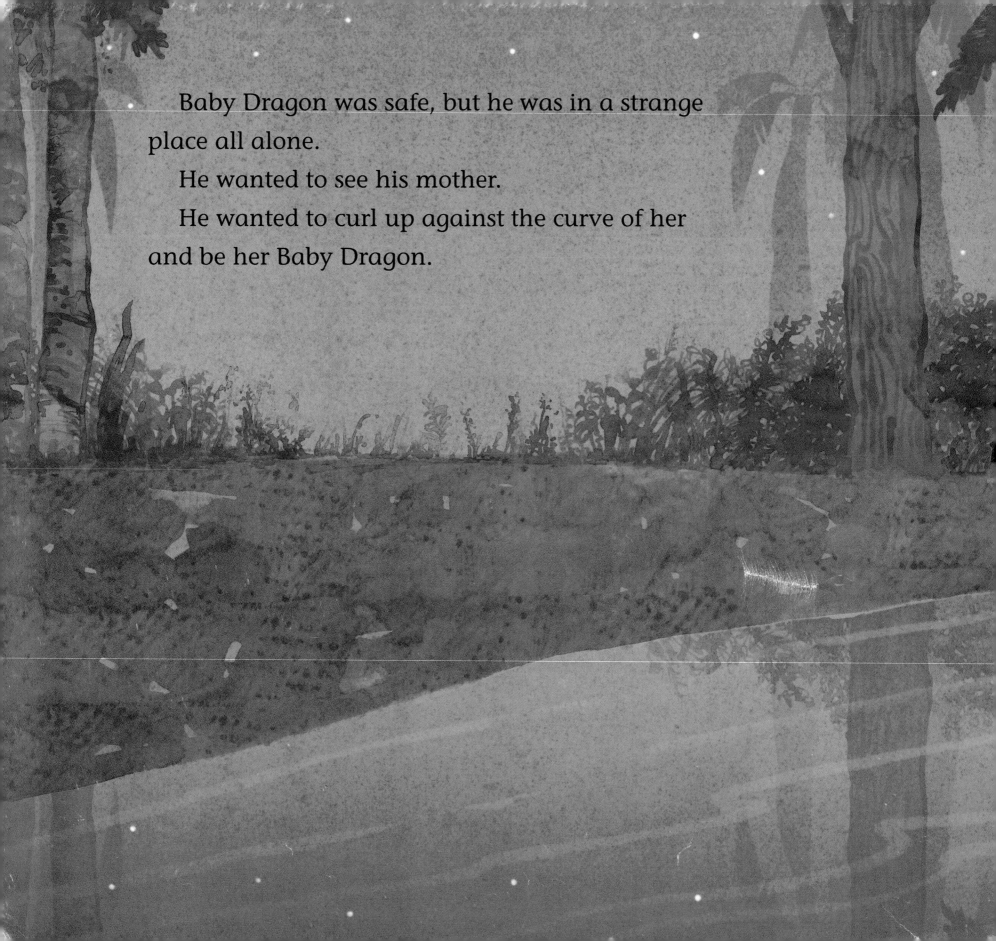

Baby Dragon was safe, but he was in a strange place all alone.

He wanted to see his mother.

He wanted to curl up against the curve of her and be her Baby Dragon.

She had told him to wait by the red fern, but he had not waited.
She said she'd be back by morning, but morning had not come.

Morning had not come! Maybe there was still time. Maybe he could go back to the red fern and his mother would be able to find him.

The stars were out. The moon was shining. Baby Dragon turned and walked back along the river, following the path of moonlight.

It was a long way, but Baby Dragon
put one foot in front of the other,

one foot in front of the other,

one foot in front of the other, until he
came to the red fern where his mother
had left him.

It was still dark.

Baby Dragon waited for morning.

He heard storks splashing in the water.

He felt the wind die down.

He watched the sky grow light.

And then his mother came.

She was very glad to see him.

Baby Dragon curled against the curve of her, and they told each other stories of their adventures.

"I missed you so much," said Baby Dragon.

"But I said I'd be back by morning," said his mother. "And now look—morning is here."

"Will you always come back?" asked Baby Dragon.

"Of course I will," she said.

Baby Dragon warmed his mother's face with his baby dragon breath.

Then he ran to find Frog. It was time to play.

To my new great-nephews: Jackson, Quinn, and Jacob

A. E.

To my friend Tom Erndt. Thank you
for drawing your dragon for me!

W. H.

First edition 2008

Library of Congress Cataloging-in-Publication Data

Ehrlich, Amy.
Baby Dragon / Amy Ehrlich ;
illustrated by Will Hillenbrand. —1st ed.
p.   cm.
Summary: All day, Baby Dragon patiently waits for his mother to return
for him, turning down other animals' offers to go play or find a snack,
but at nightfall, he agrees to go with Crocodile to find her.
ISBN 978-0-7636-2840-6
[1. Obedience—Fiction. 2. Patience—Fiction. 3. Dragons—Fiction.
4. Animals—Fiction. 5. Mother and child—Fiction.]
I. Hillenbrand, Will, ill. II. Title.
PZ7.E328Bab 2008
[E]—dc22   2007051883

2 4 6 8 10 9 7 5 3 1

Printed in Singapore

This book was typeset in Stone informal.
The illustrations were done with ink, colored pencil, finger paint, collage, and gouache on vellum.
These elements were scanned, digitally manipulated, and printed on watercolor paper.
Final details were added with colored pencil.

Candlewick Press
2067 Massachusetts Avenue
Cambridge, Massachusetts 02140

visit us at www.candlewick.com